GARY CREW

STEVEN WOOLMAN

Beneath the Surface

Beneath the Surface

Written by
GARY CREW

Illustrated by
STEVEN WOOLMAN

for Nan

Beneath the Surface is the sequel to the much-acclaimed *The Watertower*, which won the Children's Book Council Picture Book of the Year Award in 1996 and was a project very dear to the hearts of both creators. For Steven, *The Watertower* began a distinguished career as an illustrator and graphic designer, of which *Beneath the Surface* is the breathtaking culmination. Steven died while on holiday in New Zealand. The first edition of *Beneath the Surface* had only been released a matter of weeks. Sadly, he did not live to witness its favourable reception.

A Lothian Children's Book
Published in Australia and New Zealand
by Hachette Australia Pty Ltd
Level 17, 207 Kent Street,
Sydney NSW 2000
www.hachettechildrens.com.au

First published by Hodder Headline Australia
in 2004
This edition published in 2005
Reprinted in 2010, 2012, 2014

Text © Gary Crew 2004
Illustrations © Steven Woolman 2004

National Library of Australia
Cataloguing-in-Publication data

Crew, Gary, 1947- .
Beneath the surface.

For children.
ISBN 978 0 7336 1932 8.

I. Woolman, Steven. II. Title.

A823.3

Designed by Steven Woolman
Printed in China
Illustration technique: coloured pencil

Nobody in Preston could remember when the watertower
was built, or who had built it, but there it stood on Shooter's
Hill — its mighty stanchions planted deep within the earth,
its long, dark shadow stretching far across the valley.
Beyond Preston itself.
Far beyond...

From the minute he stepped off the coach, Spike knew that they were watching.

Preston's a small town, he told himself. *I'm a stranger to them now,* and picking up his bag, he headed for the hotel.

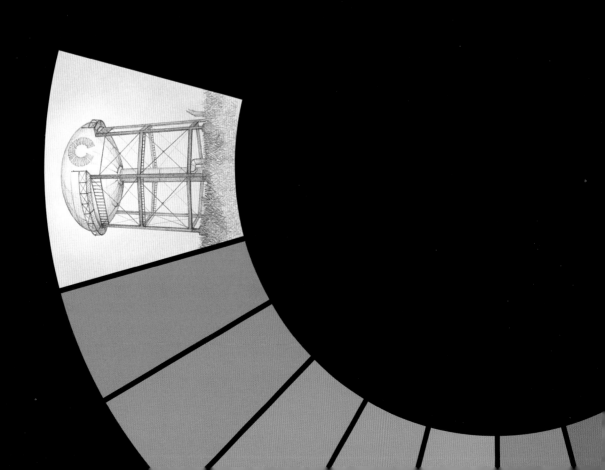

'Trotter?' the reception clerk said when he saw the name. 'There was a kid name of Spike Trotter lived 'ere once. No relation?'

Spike looked up from the register. 'Actually the name's Spiro Trotter,' he said, avoiding the question. 'Doctor Spiro Trotter.'

'Ya haven't come to set up no clinic, 'ave ya?' the clerk said. ''Cause I'm tellin' ya now, there's no one sick around here. No, sir.'

'I'm not a medical doctor,' Spike assured him. 'I'm a scientist. My degree is in Hydrology.'

'Ah, that's different then… 'Cause like I said, there's no diseases in this town. No, sir. No doctors neither. Not since…'

'I'm very tired,' Spike interrupted, 'can I have the key to my room?'

'Anyway, that Trotter kid shot through years ago,' the clerk muttered, handing him the key. 'Him and his mother likewise. Just up and left. Lost contact with 'em we did.'

Good, Spike thought, but said, pleasantly enough, 'That's life. People move on. They change.'

'They do. They certainly do,' the clerk answered. 'Bit like towns, 'eh?'

And worlds, Spike thought as he climbed the narrow stairs. *Even galaxies…*

He slept badly that night, his nightmares vivid and dreadful.

He got up early next morning and slipped away. No sooner had he entered the street than he saw that the desk clerk had been right. True, the main street seemed the same — the hotel, the service station, the shop fronts — but there was something different about the place. Now a thick and chilling mist loitered at every corner. Hung in every doorway. Dripped from every sign.

Spike couldn't remember any mist. That was not part of his childhood. Besides, how could there be, in this dust bowl? And the scientist in him stopped to make a note.

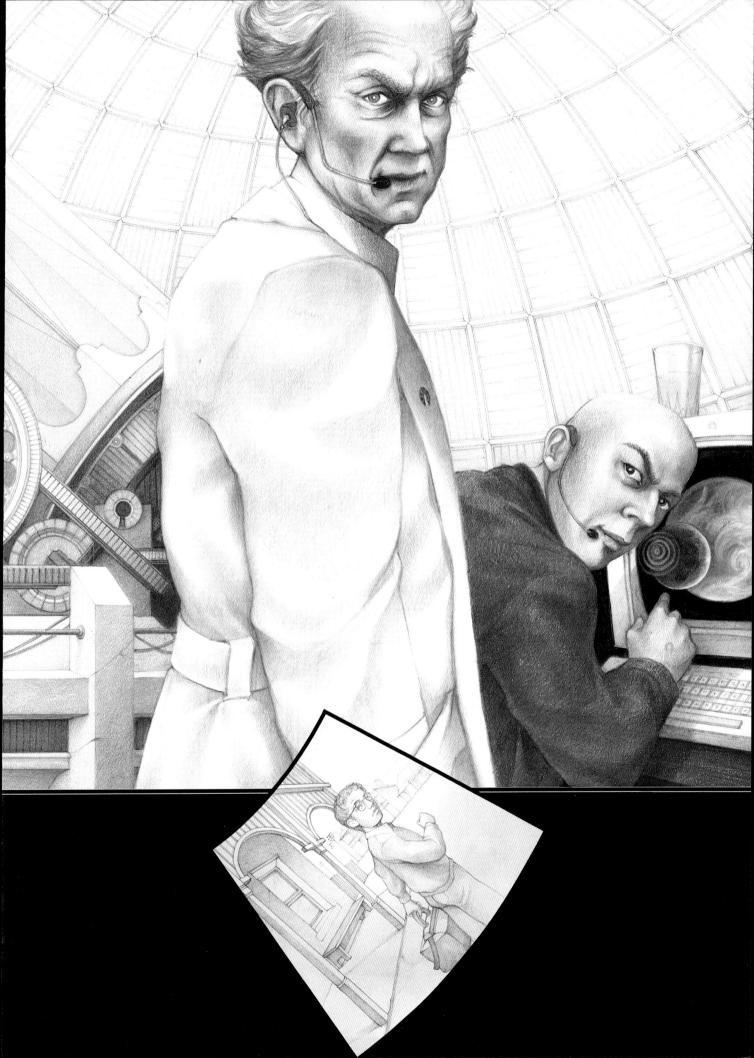

At the base of Shooter's Hill, he stopped again. The watertower had stood at the summit, he remembered. A rusty, egg-shaped monstrosity, its looming presence dominating the Preston of his childhood, and enduring still — if only in his dreams.

To see that tower again — to reaffirm its existence — and finally, to analyse its contents, was his mission.

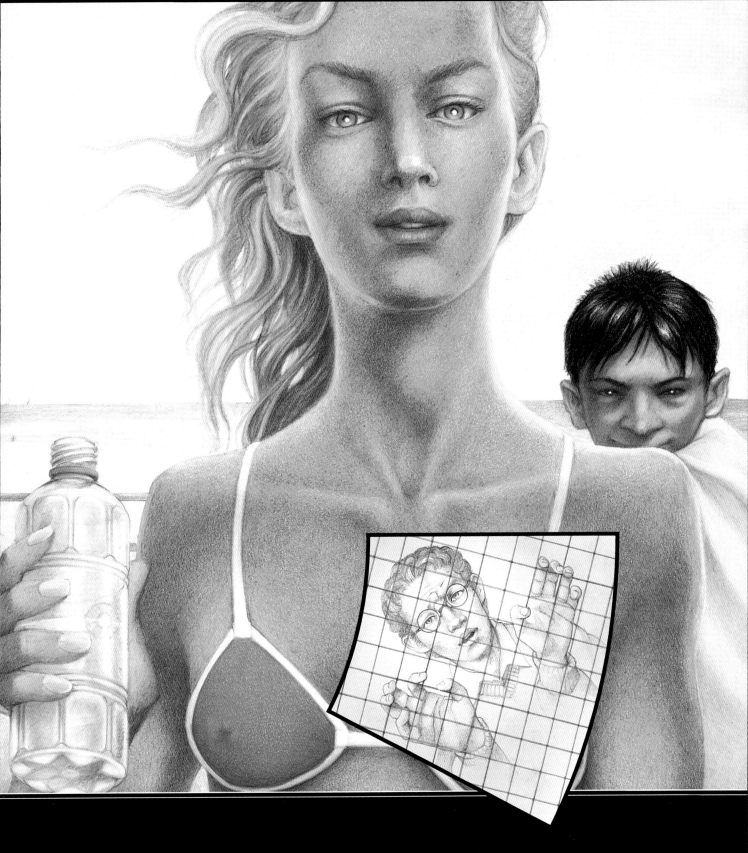

He raised his head, but could make out nothing. The hill was wreathed in mist.
And when he hit a security fence, his memory reeled. *Something's wrong,*
he thought. *The fence was at the top. I've hardly started climbing and already
I've hit wire ... unless this fence is new, which makes sense after twenty years.
Which means there's still something up there.*

Reassured, he backtracked until he found a gate. His hands roved over it, seeking a latch. He found a lock. A touch pad with lettered keys.

'Hopeless,' he sighed, punching the pad with the flat of his hand. As he did, he heard the squeak of a hinge. The gate opened as if he were expected.

The mist lifted the moment he stepped through. And there was the watertower
at the summit. His watertower. The place where he had played as a child —
laughing and hallooing; swimming and duck-diving in its dark waters.

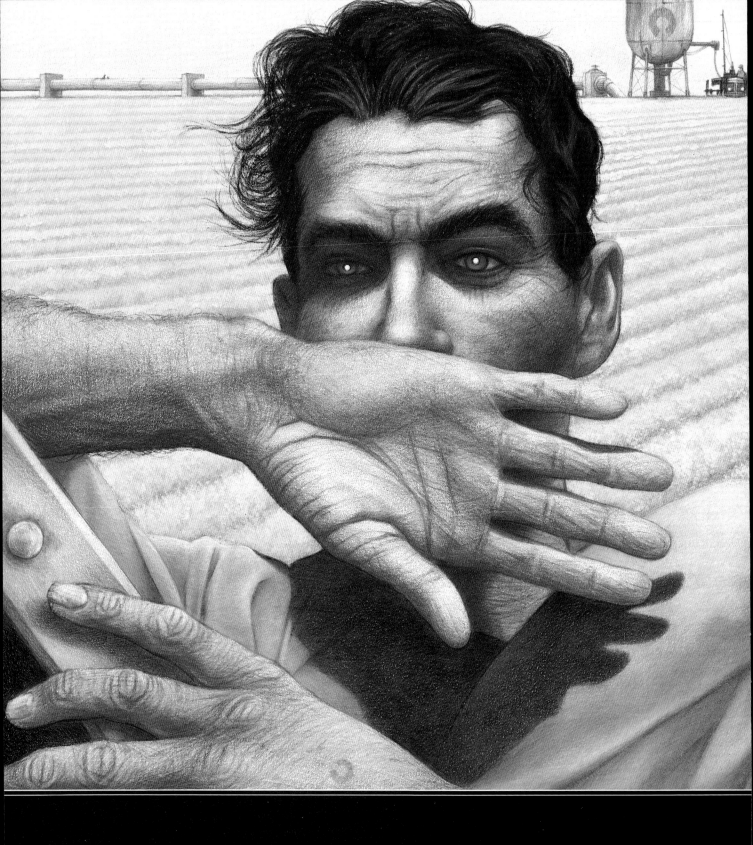

But as he drew closer, he realised that he was wrong. The tower of his childhood had been red with rust. Rotten almost. This tower was bright and gleaming, as if freshly polished.

Why would they do that? he wondered. *Unless it's to keep the water cold inside,* and he shivered, thinking of it. *And the dark…*

It's just a piece of metal, he told himself. *Always was. Always will be. Now get up there and do what you came for.*

He made his way to the ladder and began to climb.
But he did not remember it being so steep, nor so high.

And when he finally reached the top, the silvery surface looked
so smooth, so slippery, that his courage almost failed him.

What was there to be afraid of? Falling? Being pushed?

Leaving the ladder, he crawled to the centre of the tank where he reached out to grip the handle of the access hatch. Then he paused, feeling better.

He had arrived at last.

Now to get in, he thought, and heaved. But the hatch lifted easily.
Maintenance? he wondered, removing a glass vial and length of cord
from his pack.

Tucking them into his belt, he swung his legs over, located the interior
ladder, and went down.

It was dark inside. And cold. Even colder as he descended. He could
not remember the cold. Nor could he remember the vapour that drifted
on the surface below, but he went on.

Down. Down. Deeper into that murky dark.

He felt the vapour lap at his ankles. His knees, his waist, his chest.
When it reached his face, clouding his vision, he stopped. *I don't like this,*
he thought. *I'll take the sample from here.*

He took the vial from his belt and lowered it until it hit the surface and sank.
He felt the cord tighten as the vial filled, and lifted it free.

Then he went up, eager to feel the sun.

When he reached the top, he stood on the open hatch.
'There,' he said, 'I've done it. Twenty years it took, but I've done it.'

And he held the vial to the sky.

The water was clear. There was no sign of algae. He had hoped that he would
find something. Some explanation. Some reason for his fear. His nightmares

Curious, he opened his
kit and applied his tests.

Still nothing.
Not a microbe.

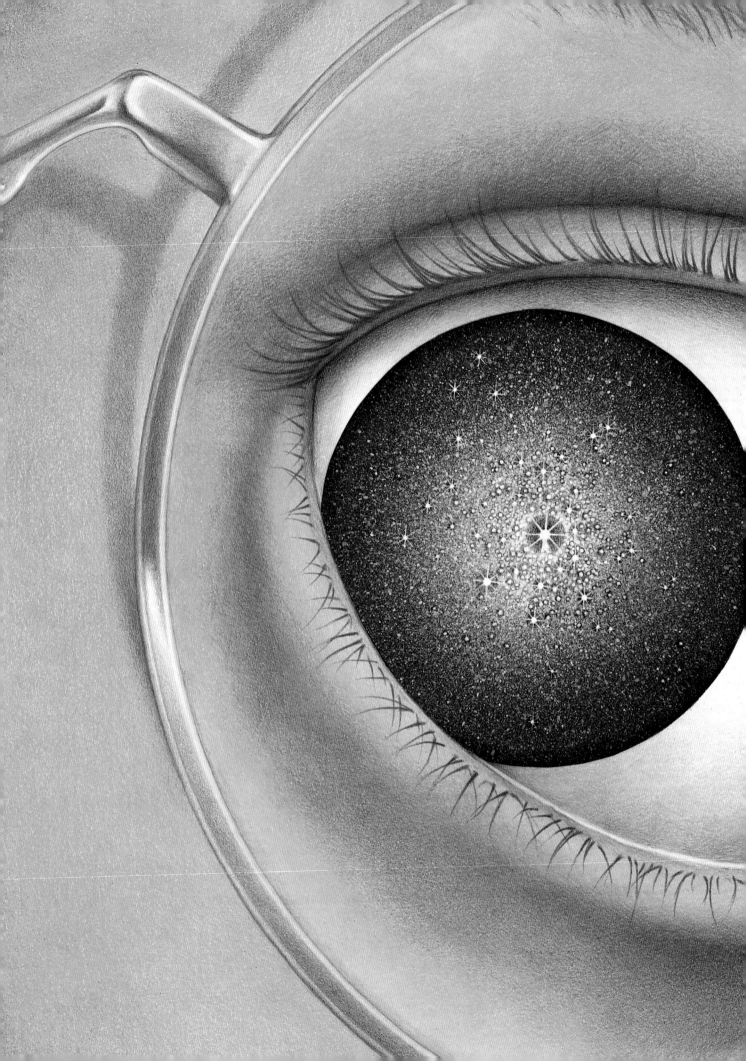

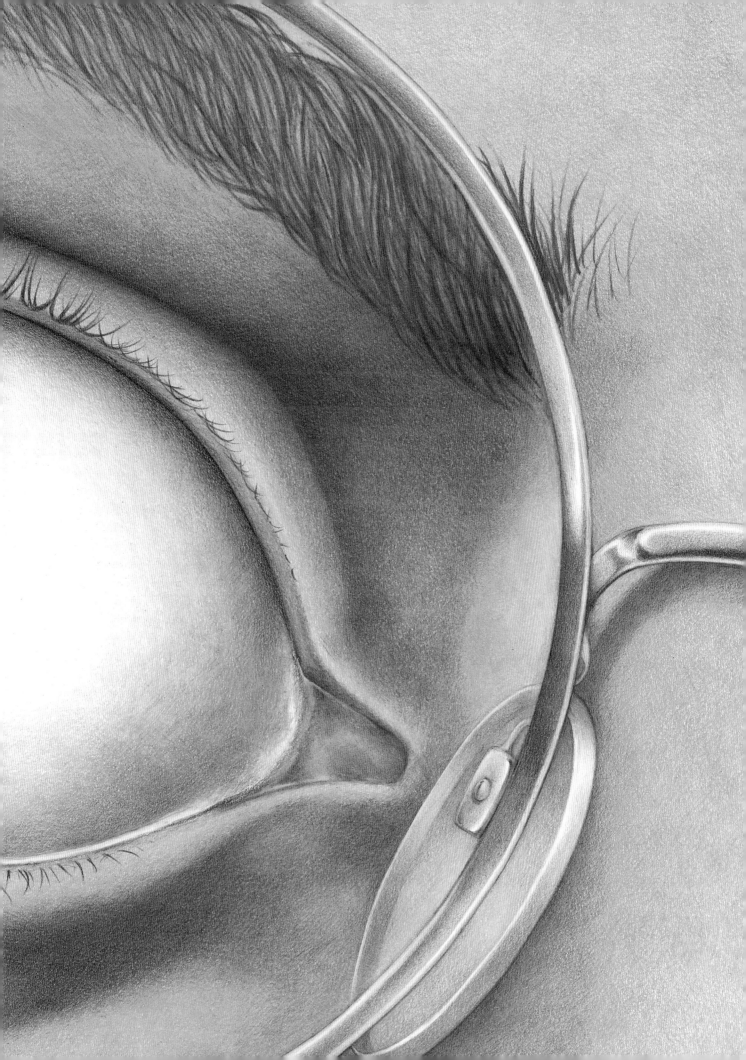

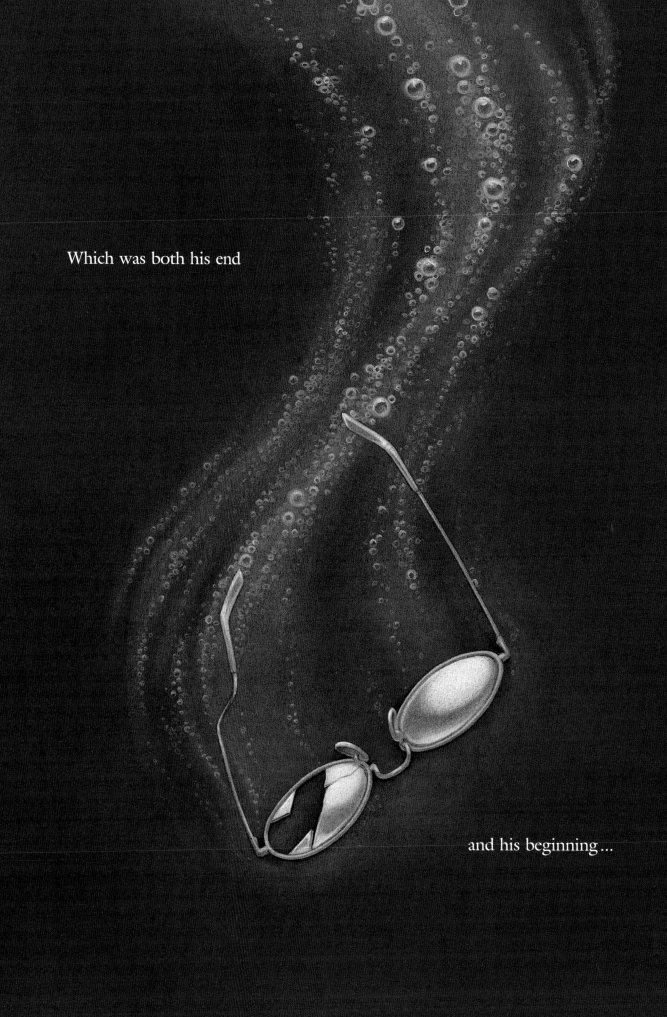

Which was both his end

and his beginning...